Lucy & Tom
Go to School

SHIRLEY HUGHES

D0258268

DUNVEGAN PRIMARY SCHOOL
BUN-SGOIL DHUN BHEAGAIN

PUFFIN BOOKS

Lucy and Tom were two little children who were not yet old enough to go to school. When it was fine they played in the garden. They liked to look over the gate and see what was happening in the street.

Often Lucy would get out her dolls and have a pretend school. Lucy was the teacher and if Tom was in a good mood he would be one of the class.

But sometimes, especially when it rained, Lucy was bored. She was tired of playing with Tom. She was tired of her toys.

Her mother said that as she was nearly five she would soon be going to a real school.

Lucy had her school things ready. She had a new grey skirt,
a pair of brown shoes, a pencil case and a satchel.
Tom wished that he had a satchel too.

Lucy and Tom knew where the school was. They had seen the boys and girls going in, and heard them shouting at playtime.

On the first day of
school Lucy held her
mother's hand very
tightly. In the school
playground there were a
great many children
waiting to go in.

They saw Lucy's friend Jane.

She was peeping out from behind her mother and holding
on to her coat.

In the cloakroom Mum
helped Lucy find her peg
and hang up her jacket.
Lucy's peg had her name
and a picture of a teddy
above it.

In the classroom
was a smiling
teacher. She was
writing down
names.

She said, "Hello,
Lucy! Hello, Jane!"
She was called Miss
Walker.

The classroom was full of
children and a great
many interesting things
to look at. There was a
little shop with pretend
money.

Lucy and Jane started to play
in the shop with three other
little girls.

The mothers watched for a while. When it was time for them to go and get on with *their* shopping Jane did not want them to leave.

Lucy's mother gave her a hug and said, "See you at dinner time. Look after Jane, won't you?"

Lucy wasn't feeling specially brave, but she took Jane's hand. Tom yelled on the way out because *he* wanted to go to school too.

At playtime Lucy had some milk with a straw.

The playground was very noisy. Some children were playing games. Some were fighting, some were chasing about and some were walking with their arms round each other.

Jane had an apple. She gave Lucy a bite and they had a quiet game in a corner.

After playtime Miss Walker read a story. They thought she was a very nice teacher indeed.

Later Lucy sorted some shells and coloured a picture.

"What did you do this morning, now I am a schoolgirl?"
Lucy asked Tom at dinner time. Tom had done some
colouring too.

Lucy's best thing at school was music and movement. She liked pretending to be a tiny mouse and then growing into a huge giant.

She liked it when they dressed up and acted their stories.

She liked Assembly too, because of the hymns.

Lucy's worst thing at
school was a boy
called Neil Bailey, who
kept pushing her in
the playground.

Some days Lucy
looked forward to
going to school and
some days she did not
want to go very much,
but she soon got used
to it.

Now Tom was bored at home. He missed Lucy and she was often too tired to play when she came home from school. He followed Mum about wanting something to do.

Mum said that Tom could
join a playgroup in the
mornings. She bought him
a satchel just like Lucy's.
He put into it some pencils
and cars and his old
Teddy.

At the playgroup Tom painted and sang and played with toys and clay. There were plenty of boys and girls there to be his friends.

Tom liked the playgroup so much that he ran ahead of Mum every morning to get there first. Now Tom was a schoolboy too!

PUFFIN BOOKS

Published by the Penguin Group: London, New York,
Australia, Canada and New Zealand
Penguin Books Ltd, Registered Offices: Harmondsworth, Middlesex, England

First published by Victor Gollancz Ltd 1973
Published in Picture Puffins 1992
7 9 10 8
Copyright © Shirley Hughes, 1973
All rights reserved

Made and printed in Italy by Printers srl – Trento